CLASSIC TALES

Jack
and the
Beanstalk

Alexis Roumanis

FICTION READALONG
AV2 BY WEIGL™
ADDED VALUE • AUDIO VISUAL

Your AV² Media Enhanced book gives you a fiction readalong online. Log on to www.av2books.com and enter the unique book code from this page to use your readalong.

AV² Readalong Navigation

HIGHLIGHTED TEXT   HOME 🏠   CLOSE ✕

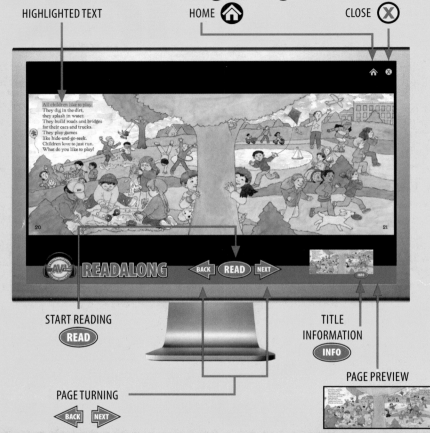

Go to **www.av2books.com**, and enter this book's unique code.

BOOK CODE

W 9 4 7 4 5 7

AV² by Weigl brings you media enhanced books that support active learning.

START READING
READ

TITLE INFORMATION
INFO

PAGE PREVIEW

PAGE TURNING
BACK **NEXT**

Published by AV² by Weigl
350 5ᵗʰ Avenue, 59ᵗʰ Floor New York, NY 10118
Websites: www.av2books.com

Library of Congress Control Number: 2016930576

ISBN 978-1-4896-5242-3 (Hardcover)
ISBN 978-1-4896-5244-7 (Multi-user eBook)

Copyright ©2008 by Kyowon Co., Ltd.
First published in 2008 by Kyowon Co., Ltd.

Printed in the United States of America in Brainerd, Minnesota
1 2 3 4 5 6 7 8 9 0   20 19 18 17 16

032016
012916

There once was a lively boy called Jack.

He lived in a poor village with his mother.

"I can't get any milk out of the cow," said Jack.

"She's too old," said his mother.
"Go and sell her in the market."

"How much should I sell her for?" he asked.

"No less than five gold pieces," said
his mother. "Bring the money straight
home when she is sold."

While Jack was walking the cow
to the market, he met an old man.

"Where are you going, boy?"
asked the old man.

"To the market, sir," replied Jack.

"Strange that you are taking your cow
to the market," muttered the old man.

"My mother told me to sell her," said Jack.

"Really?" he mumbled.
"I'll buy her from you."

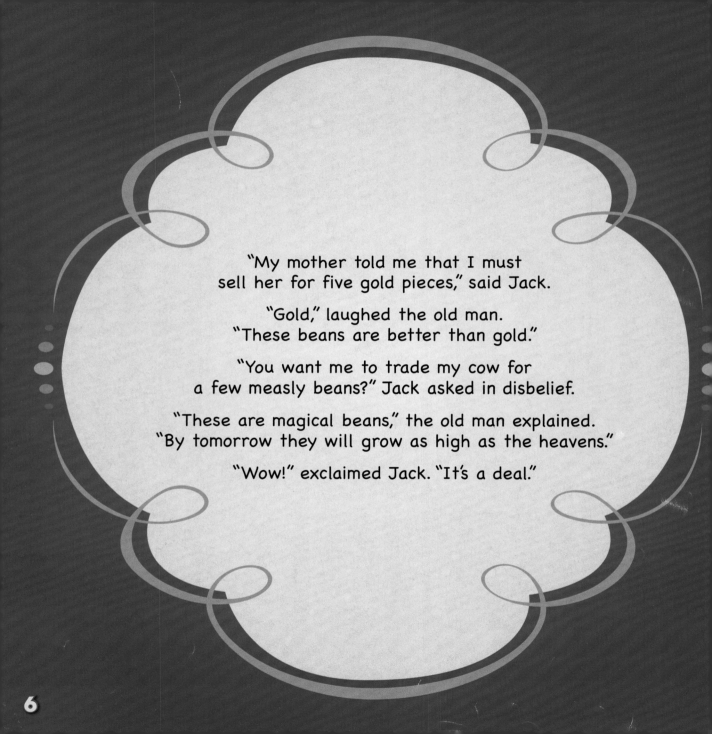

"My mother told me that I must
sell her for five gold pieces," said Jack.

"Gold," laughed the old man.
"These beans are better than gold."

"You want me to trade my cow for
a few measly beans?" Jack asked in disbelief.

"These are magical beans," the old man explained.
"By tomorrow they will grow as high as the heavens."

"Wow!" exclaimed Jack. "It's a deal."

When Jack returned home,
his mother was furious.

"You sold the cow for only five beans!" she yelled.

"But they are magical beans," Jack explained.

"Nonsense," his mother scoffed, throwing
the beans into the garden.

The next morning though, Jack was shocked to
see a giant beanstalk in the garden.

"The old man was right," said Jack excitedly.
"I wonder what is at the top of it?"

He began to climb the beanstalk.

When Jack reached the top
of the beanstalk, he looked down.

"Everything looks so small
down there," he gasped.

When Jack looked up again, he noticed
a giant house sitting on the clouds.

"I wonder if they have something to eat,"
he thought. "I haven't eaten breakfast yet."

Jack walked to the house
and knocked on the front door.

11

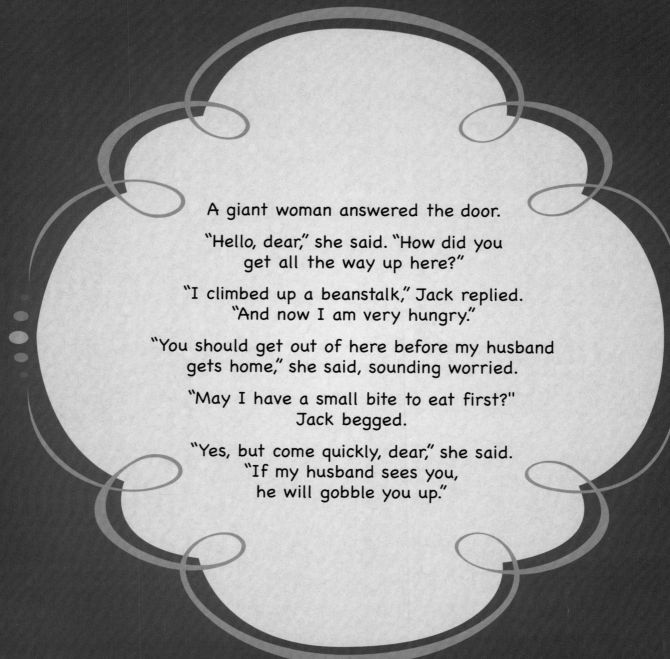

A giant woman answered the door.

"Hello, dear," she said. "How did you
get all the way up here?"

"I climbed up a beanstalk," Jack replied.
"And now I am very hungry."

"You should get out of here before my husband
gets home," she said, sounding worried.

"May I have a small bite to eat first?"
Jack begged.

"Yes, but come quickly, dear," she said.
"If my husband sees you,
he will gobble you up."

The giant woman gave Jack
some tarts and milk.

"These are delicious," said Jack.

He was nearly finished when he
heard a loud thump.

"My husband is home," cried the large
woman. "You must hide in here."

She pushed Jack into a very big oven.

"I'm hungry!" bellowed the giant.

Jack trembled with fear.

"What's that smell coming from the oven?"
the giant boomed. "It smells delicious."

"It's the smell of the lunch I made you," said his
wife. "I've cooked two lambs for your lunch."

The giant sat at the table
and gulped down his food.

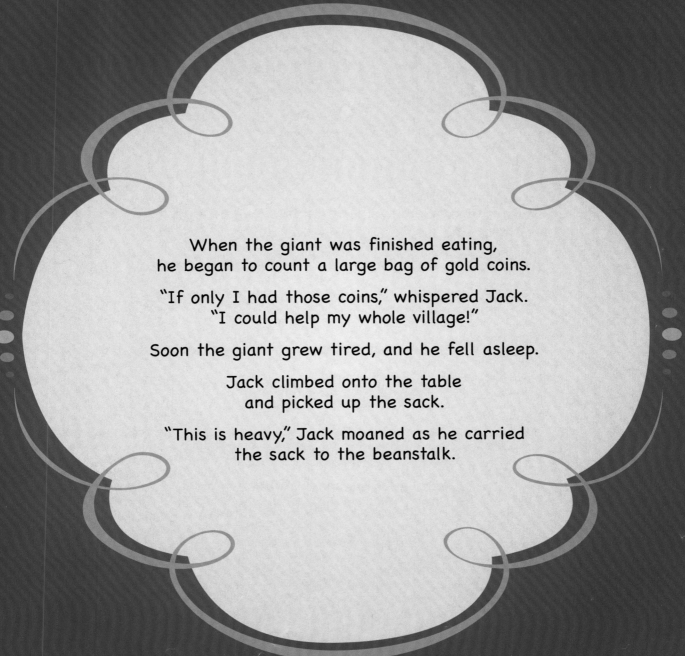

When the giant was finished eating,
he began to count a large bag of gold coins.

"If only I had those coins," whispered Jack.
"I could help my whole village!"

Soon the giant grew tired, and he fell asleep.

Jack climbed onto the table
and picked up the sack.

"This is heavy," Jack moaned as he carried
the sack to the beanstalk.

It took Jack a long time to climb down the beanstalk with the heavy sack of gold.

"Where have you been?" Jack's mother cried.

"I climbed the beanstalk," said Jack proudly.

"I can't believe you were right about the beans being magical," his mother said.

"We are rich!" Jack announced, setting the sack of gold on the table.

"Where did you find all of this gold?" asked his mother, amazed.

Jack told his mother all about his adventure in the clouds.

The next day, Jack climbed
back up the beanstalk.

"You've come back," said the giant's wife, shocked.

"I came back for more tarts," Jack lied.
"They were delicious."

"Why, thank you," she replied, beaming.

"May I have some more?" Jack asked.

The huge woman nodded.

"Hurry up, then," she said.

As Jack was eating the tarts he heard
the loud thump of the giant.

"Quick, hide in the oven," urged the giant's wife.

"Bring me my hen," the giant bellowed.

His wife placed the small hen on the table.

"Hen, lay me a golden egg at once,"
ordered the giant.

The hen laid an egg made of solid gold.

"I must have that hen," Jack whispered.
"My village will be the richest place
in the kingdom."

"I'm hungry," boomed the giant.

"I have three goats for you today,
my dear," his wife replied.

When the giant had finished eating,
he fell fast asleep.

Jack climbed onto the table
and picked up the hen.

He climbed back down the beanstalk
carrying the hen under one arm.

"Look, Mother," said Jack excitedly.
"I found a magical hen."

"What does it do?" his mother asked.

"Watch this," said Jack.
"Dear hen, lay me a golden egg."

The hen laid an egg made of solid gold.

"Oh my," gasped Jack's mother.
"Now we will never run out of gold."

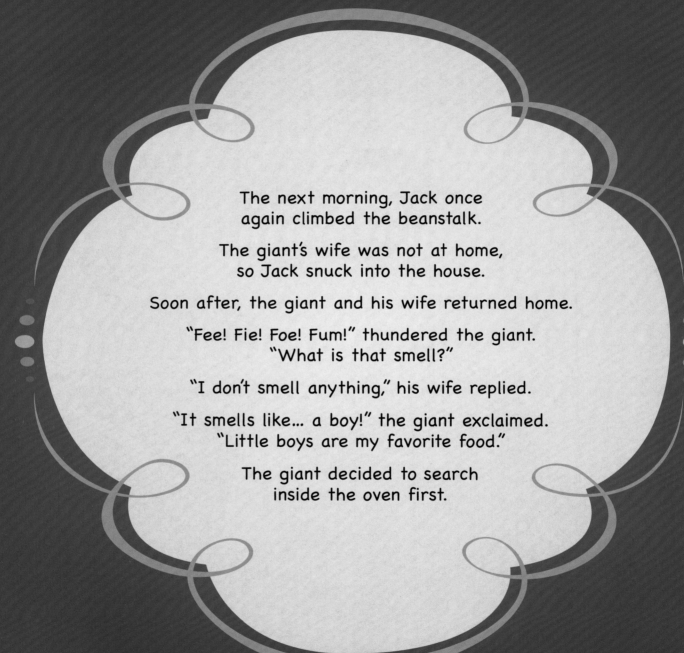

The next morning, Jack once
again climbed the beanstalk.

The giant's wife was not at home,
so Jack snuck into the house.

Soon after, the giant and his wife returned home.

"Fee! Fie! Foe! Fum!" thundered the giant.
"What is that smell?"

"I don't smell anything," his wife replied.

"It smells like... a boy!" the giant exclaimed.
"Little boys are my favorite food."

The giant decided to search
inside the oven first.

The giant sniffed inside the oven,
but could not find anything.

"You must be smelling that cow I cooked for lunch,"
said the giant's wife.

Jack peeked over the edge of the large pot he had
jumped into. "I am glad I hid in here," he thought.

"No, I am sure that is the smell of a boy,"
roared the giant.

The giant searched the house, but could not find Jack.

"Why don't you sit down and eat
your lunch?" said the giant's wife.

"Very well," the giant answered,
"But bring me my harp so I can listen
to music while I eat."

33

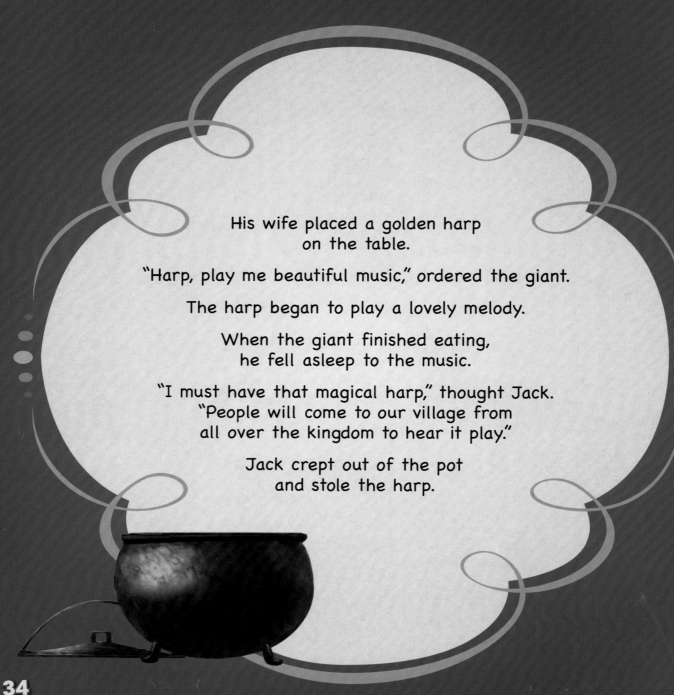

His wife placed a golden harp
on the table.

"Harp, play me beautiful music," ordered the giant.

The harp began to play a lovely melody.

When the giant finished eating,
he fell asleep to the music.

"I must have that magical harp," thought Jack.
"People will come to our village from
all over the kingdom to hear it play."

Jack crept out of the pot
and stole the harp.

Jack barely made it to the door,
when the giant awoke with a start.

"Where is my harp?" he thundered.

The giant spotted Jack and chased him
all the way to the beanstalk.

"Come back, thief!" the giant shouted.

Jack climbed down the beanstalk
as fast as his legs could carry him.

"I will catch you, boy," yelled the giant.

Jack looked up to see the giant following him down the beanstalk.

"I must hurry," gasped Jack.

The beanstalk began to shake from the weight of the giant.

When Jack was near the bottom, he cried out "Mother, bring me my axe! Please hurry!"

Jack's mother quickly handed him
the axe when he reached the ground.

"Stand back," ordered Jack. "I must cut down this
beanstalk before the giant reaches us."

Jack swung his axe wildly at the beanstalk.

"Hurry, son!" said his mother, trembling.
"The giant is almost here."

Jack took one last swing,
and the beanstalk began to fall.

"Jack, move back!"
yelled his mother, panicking.

Jack jumped back from the falling beanstalk.

The giant shook the earth when his body hit the ground. He did not move again.

"Hooray!" exclaimed Jack, "I did it!"

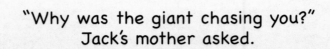

"Why was the giant chasing you?"
Jack's mother asked.

"I took this harp from his house," said Jack.

"But you can't play the harp," replied his Mother,
looking confused.

"Harp," said Jack, smiling.
"Play me some beautiful music."

To his mother's delight, the harp played
a wonderful melody.

Jack and his mother danced to the music.

Now that Jack was rich, the most beautiful girl
in his village agreed to marry him.

Many people came from all over the kingdom
to hear the story of the giant.

They also came to hear the beautiful music
of the magical harp.

Jack shared the giant's riches with his entire village.

They all lived happily ever after.

Benjamin Tabart was born in 1767 in England. He was an English publisher and bookseller in London. Tabart published a list of books in a series called the Juvenile Library, many of which were written by himself. At the time, it was common to publish children's stories that focused on strong morals. Tabart incorporated these morals into *Jack and the Beanstalk*.

Tabart was the first to publish *Jack and the Beanstalk* in 1807. He based his story on *The Story of Jack Spriggins and the Enchanted Bean*, which was first published in 1734. Tabart succeeded in popularizing the story to a wide audience.

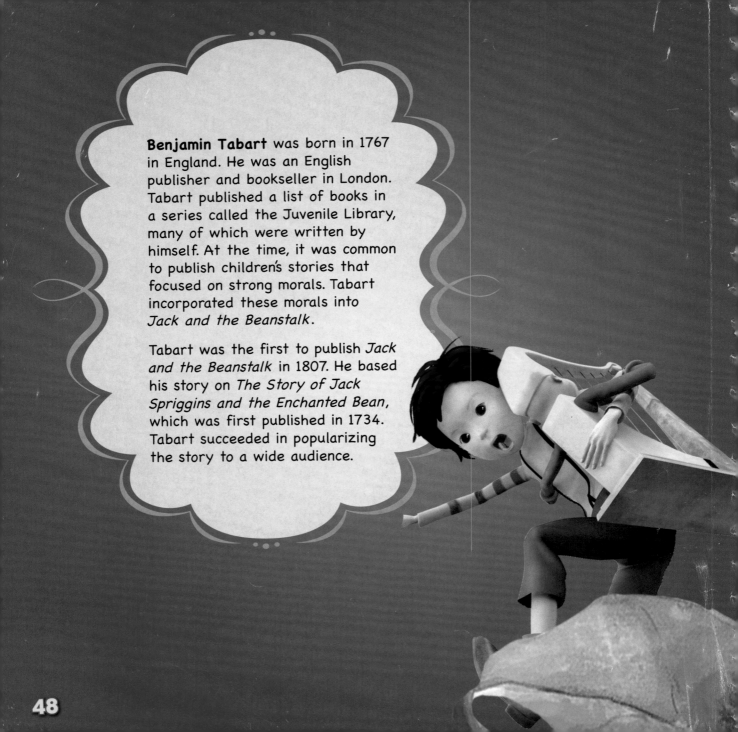